"Hi! Um...are you Claire? I saw you yesterday, and I thought you looked really nice and friendly."

Claire felt so happy. She was sure now that she really was the one Lauren wanted to be friends with.

ORCHARD BOOKS
96 Leonard Street, London EC2A 4XD
Orchard Books Australia
Unit 31/56 O'Riordan Street, Alexandria, NSW 2015
First published in Great Britain in 2002
A PAPERBACK ORIGINAL
Text © Ann Bryant 2002
Series conceived and created by Ann Bryant
Series consultant Anne Finnis
The right of Ann Bryant to be identified as the author
of this work has been asserted by her in accordance with the
Copyright, Designs and Patents Act, 1988.
A CIP catalogue record for this book is available
from the British Library.
ISBN 1 84121 790 5
3 5 7 9 10 8 6 4 2
Printed in Great Britain

Make Friends With
Claire

Ann Bryant

ORCHARD BOOKS

Chapter One

Claire stood very still. It helped her to concentrate. She knew she mustn't whine or sound grumpy, otherwise her mum would say that Izzie *definitely* couldn't come on holiday with them. Claire had already asked once and been told, "No, we're taking your cousin, Harriet, as usual." But maybe if Claire asked in a really polite, grown-up way, her mum might just change her mind.

"Mum," began Claire carefully, "you

know how Izzie is my best friend?"

Claire's mum narrowed her eyes and spoke in a suspicious voice, as though she knew exactly what was coming next. "Uh huh…"

"Well pleeeeease can she come on holiday with us instead of Harriet? Pleeeeease."

"No, because I've already asked Auntie Kate if Harriet can come. And anyway you and Harriet had a great time last year."

Claire forgot about being polite and grown-up. "I know we did. But I've only seen her a few times since then. And I just know Izzie and I would have an absolutely brilliant time."

Claire's mum sighed and tipped her head on one side. "I'm sorry, Claire. I'm not changing my mind. You can't invite

someone to come away on holiday with you and then phone up and say, 'Oh sorry, you can't come actually, because there's someone we want more than you!'"

"Harriet would never find out if we pretended we weren't going on holiday after all."

"That doesn't sound like *my* daughter talking," said her mum, frowning at Claire.

Claire went a bit pink and looked down. She knew she was being horrible to poor Harriet.

"I *do* like Harriet," she said quietly. "Just not as much as Izzie."

"I know you do," said her mum, smiling. "I think I'll phone Auntie Kate right now, because I never did tell her the exact dates. I just said somewhere

near the end of the school holidays."

Claire sat down at the kitchen table and looked at the TV guide. Most of the time she didn't mind not having any brothers and sisters. It was only when they were going away on holiday that she thought how lucky her friends were. They all had at least one other person in their family to play with, even if it was only a baby.

"Hi Kate, it's me!" said her mum into the phone. "I said I'd let you know our holiday dates. It's the eleventh to the eighteenth…" There was a silence while Mum listened to Kate's reply. It seemed to be going on rather a long time. Claire looked up. Her mum was frowning in a thoughtful way. "Oh right… Yes… I see… Well…it can't be helped. Don't worry. It's my own fault. I should have

let you know earlier..."

Claire felt a butterfly in her stomach – not the nervous sort – the happy sort. She sat up straight and listened intently to see if there were any more clues. "No, no, no. It won't put us out at all, really. I'm sure Claire can think of another friend who might be able to come along..."

At that point Claire's mum looked up and gave Claire a smile that said "Aren't you the lucky one?"

And Claire just smiled back, even though she really felt like jumping up and down, punching the air and shouting "Yesssss!" at the top of her voice.

It was nearly bedtime. Claire was in her room. Her suitcase was packed but the

lid was open. Izzie had been round to play in the morning and the two girls had made a list of everything they were going to take with them to the holiday village. Claire couldn't stop looking at all her clothes folded neatly in the suitcase. She was dying for the next day to arrive. She was even going to bed early to make it come sooner.

The phone was ringing downstairs. Claire got into bed and looked at the picture in the brochure of the lodge where they would be staying. She couldn't wait to show Izzie the Kids' Centre. It had been such fun last year with Harriet. And with Izzie…

Her mum came into her room as she was looking at the photo of the swimming pool. Claire took one look at her mum's serious face and knew straight

away that something was wrong.

"I'm afraid Izzie's gone down with chicken pox, love. She's not going to be able to come after all."

Claire felt like bursting into tears. She couldn't think what to say, so she just stared at the brochure, her eyes full of tears. Her mum sat on the bed and put her arm round Claire.

"You can still go to the Kids' Centre," she said gently. "It'll be just as much fun because you'll make new friends."

"I don't want any new friends," said Claire, shaking her mum's arm off her. She wanted to be hugged really, but the big disappointment was making her cross and upset.

"I'm sure you'll feel differently when you actually get to the Centre. There are so many fun things to do, aren't there?

Playing games, dancing, swimming…"

Claire slid down under the bedclothes because however cross she was, she still didn't want her mum to hear her next words. "I bet it'll be the worst holiday ever!"

Chapter Two

The journey in the car was long and boring.

"Let's play Pubs' Legs," said Claire's dad.

"I don't feel like it," said Claire.

She did really, it was just that she and Izzie had planned to play Pubs' Legs on the journey and it wouldn't be the same with her dad. Claire was going to take one side of the road and Izzie the other. Whenever they saw a pub sign they

would count the number of legs in the name. You'd score two for The King William and four for The Golden Lion.

"We could play Registration Plates," said Claire's mum.

"I'm listening to my music," said Claire, sinking down into her seat with her Walkman on.

Claire saw her mum and dad exchange a look. She knew she was being a baby but she couldn't help it. Then it began to rain, so now the sadness seemed to be on the outside as well as the inside of Claire.

When they arrived at the holiday village and Claire saw the lodge where they'd be staying, she couldn't help feeling a teeny bit excited.

"Let's go swimming straight away," she said to her mum and dad. Her dad

laughed. "Don't you want to unpack first?"

About an hour later Claire was diving down to the bottom of the swimming pool, picking up coins that her dad had deliberately dropped for her.

"You're pretty good at that!" someone called out from the side. Claire looked up to see a smiley young woman wearing jeans and a red T-shirt. "I'm Lisa. I'm just off home, but I'll be here tomorrow if you're coming to the Kids' Centre."

"I might," said Claire.

"Have you been before?" asked Lisa.

Claire nodded. "Last year."

"Great! It's a really busy week. It's going to be packed."

"Will there be aerobics?" asked Claire. That had been her favourite thing last year.

"There certainly will!" said Lisa. "And there's a new trampoline too! See you tomorrow then!"

Claire smiled. "OK."

And as she plunged down to the bottom to pick up a coin, she thought to herself, maybe the holiday won't be so bad after all.

The next morning Claire and her mum and dad went into the town. They looked round the market, went into the museum and the shopping precinct, then had lunch in a really nice café, where the ice-creams were the biggest Claire had ever seen.

"Mum and I thought we'd go on a long walk this afternoon," said Claire's dad. "Do you want to come with us or do you want to go to the Kids' Centre?"

Claire had been thinking about the Kids' Centre all morning. The more she'd thought about it the more nervous she'd felt. It was what Lisa had said about it being packed. Everyone was sure to be there with their brothers and sisters or their friends. And Claire would probably be the only one on her own. But then she remembered that there were always quite a few people supervising. And Lisa did seem very nice and friendly. She'd probably make sure Claire wasn't lonely.

Claire nodded slowly. "OK, I'll try it," she said finally.

Chapter Three

The Kids' Centre *was* packed. Claire stood next to Lisa and stared round wondering what to do first. The swimming pool was on the other side of a glass partition. She could see a boy climbing on to one of the supervisor's shoulders. He shouted something excitedly and the supervisor laughed and swung him into the air. Down he came with a splosh.

Claire's eyes wandered back to what was going on around her in the Kids'

Centre. She watched some younger children giggling as they clambered over plastic mats and through tunnels. They looked very hot. Then she looked at the trampoline. A girl with frizzy hair was doing somersaults and all sorts of clever jumps on it. Claire thought she might have a go when no one was watching. She'd done it once before when Izzie had had a trampoline party and everyone had said she was really good at it.

"Do you want to play Crazy Ladders with Nick?" asked Lisa, pointing to a game that one of the helpers had organised on mats near the café section.

Claire saw that the children were all in pairs and shook her head quickly. She thought everyone would stare at her if she went to join in on her own. Then they'd stare even more when Nick had

to stop the game to explain it to Claire.

"What about guessing how many sweets there are in this jar?" asked Lisa. "There's a prize for the winner."

"I guessed sixty-four."

Lisa turned to see who had spoken. It was the girl with frizzy hair who was bouncing on the trampoline. "Can you do backwards somersaults?" she called out. "I can. Watch!"

Claire watched. She knew she'd never be able to do a backwards somersault, even if she practised for the whole holiday.

"That's really good," said Claire.

Lisa smiled. "Why don't you let Claire have a go now, Amelia?"

"I will in a minute," said Amelia, a scowl appearing on her face.

"No, come on, you've had lots of goes…"

"I'll just guess how many sweets there are first," said Claire, because Amelia didn't look at all pleased about having to get off the trampoline.

"Lisa, we need another ball," an older boy called out from the ping-pong table.

"Ask Chris," called Lisa.

"He's helping on the pool table."

"Well ask someone else."

"They're all busy," said the boy. So Lisa had to go. "I'll be back in a minute, Claire."

Amelia stood next to Claire. "You're not allowed to guess sixty-four," she said. Claire wished she'd go away. She was quite tall and was probably about the same age as Claire. But it was hard to tell because she was standing like a grown-up, with one leg bent, her hip sticking out and her arms folded.

21

"What do you guess then?" she asked Claire.

"I haven't finished counting," said Claire.

Another girl came along. "What's *her* name?" she asked Amelia.

"Claire," said Amelia. Then she dropped her voice to a whisper. "My brother could work it out quicker than her and he's only four."

The other girl didn't reply but Claire could feel her staring. "Have you come with anyone?" she asked.

Claire shook her head.

"D'you like ping-pong?"

Claire shook her head again.

"D'you like trampolining?"

Claire wasn't sure what to say. "A bit."

"Go on then. Show us."

"I'm doing this," said Claire, feeling

relieved because she could see Lisa rushing back with a clipboard.

"Sorry about that," she said, "What do you guess, Claire?"

"Three hundred and fifty-five," said Claire.

Amelia and the other girl turned their backs and started giggling. Lisa didn't notice. She was concentrating on writing down Claire's guess. "Me and Steph'll look after Claire," said Amelia, giving Lisa a big smile.

"Oh that's nice!" said Lisa.

Claire wanted to tell Lisa not to leave her but of course she couldn't. That would have made her seem like a big baby. So she watched sadly as Lisa hurried off towards the swimming pool, wishing she could hurry off too – as far away from the Kids' Centre as possible.

Chapter Four

"I'm going swimming actually," Claire said to Amelia.

She started to walk off.

"You can go swimming in a minute," said Amelia, as though she was the boss. "First you've got to show me and Steph what you can do on the trampoline."

"I've only done it once before," said Claire. "I'm not really much good at it."

"It's dead easy," said Steph. "Look."

She kicked off her trainers and jumped

on to the trampoline. Claire had just caught sight of a big notice. She read it.

DO NOT GO ON THE TRAMPOLINE UNLESS A MEMBER OF STAFF IS PRESENT.

"You're not allowed," said Claire. "Look, it says."

"That's for the little ones," said Steph, getting off. "Me and Amelia go on it whenever we want. You can too. Go on."

Claire's knees were trembling. Maybe if she just had a quick go, Amelia and Steph would stop pestering her. She took her trainers off and climbed on. It was only three steps to the middle but her legs were so shaky that she fell over. Claire laughed at herself to show Steph and Amelia that she wasn't bothered. Then, very carefully, looking down at her feet, she started doing

small bounces. Nothing went wrong so she bounced a little higher. It felt easy, just like when she'd been at Izzie's party that time. In fact Claire even thought she might try a somersault later when the other two weren't watching.

Then, right in the middle of her thoughts, a man's voice boomed out, "Hey! Off that trampoline! What does the sign say?"

Claire's heart thumped loudly as she stopped bouncing. She looked round. Steph and Amelia were nowhere to be seen. But one of the supervisors was striding towards her with a cross look on his face, and the game of Crazy Ladders had completely stopped because everyone was too busy staring at Claire.

It was on the tip of Claire's tongue to say, "Steph said it was OK for me to

have a go," but then she changed her mind. Steph and Amelia had tricked her on purpose. If the man told them off they might be even more horrible to her.

"Sorry," said Claire. "I didn't see it."

The man looked as though he felt a bit sorry for her then. He wagged his finger but grinned to show he was only pretending to be cross. "If we made the sign any bigger it'd go up to the ceiling!"

Claire smiled and said sorry again as she started to scramble off.

"That's all right," the man said. "You can stay on it now I'm here. My name's Chris. What's yours?"

"Claire."

"Okey-dokey, Claire. Get bouncing then!"

So Claire did. She didn't quite dare do a somersault but she did star jumps and

tucks and twists. It was great. She could have stayed there all afternoon. Chris chatted to her while she bounced. Once, when she glanced over to the café, she noticed Amelia and Steph eating crisps and watching her. Steph said something to Amelia behind her hand but Claire just ignored them. She felt safe with Chris.

Suddenly some loud music came on.

"Time for aerobics," said Chris. "Come on, it's great fun. Lisa and I are the leaders."

Claire wished she didn't have to stop trampolining, but she had no choice because Chris was going. Still, aerobics was great fun. Or at least it would be as long as Amelia and Steph didn't join in. Over in the café they were chucking their crisp packets in the bin. Claire's heart sank.

W.H.SMITH RETAIL LTD
SOUTH GYLE
TELEPHONE NO: 0131 317 1771

VAT REG NO: 238 5548 36
Thank You For Shopping With Us
Cashier: KIRSTEN KERR

	£
BRYANT,MAKE FRIENDS	3.99
1 BAL DUE	3.99
CASH	5.00
CHANGE	1.01

3588 002 03 3170 12:44 26DEC02

Save as you spend with

WHSmith CLUBCARD

Chapter Five

Everyone in the Kids' Centre had stopped what they were doing to come and join in with the aerobics class. Even Steph and Amelia, worst luck. Claire stood at the back as far away from them as possible. Lisa and Chris were wearing headsets with microphones so their voices could be heard over the loud music.

"OK, let's shake it all out!" called Lisa, in a bright, bubbly voice. She'd changed into a purple crop top and purple shorts.

"Start with your hands."

"Go for it!" said Chris in the same enthusiastic voice.

All the children shook their hands in time with the music. Then Lisa and Chris had them jumping up and down, twisting and shaking like mad. Everyone was laughing. Claire laughed too, but she wasn't really enjoying it all that much, because she was worrying about Amelia and Steph. They'd been right at the front when the class had started but now they were in the middle. Claire kept an eye on them. She could tell that they were purposely making their way gradually further and further back. By the time the warm-up music had finished and Lisa was telling everyone to stand with their feet apart ready for the dance, Amelia and Steph had shuffled their way behind Claire, to the very back.

"We've been working on the dance for the last few days," called Lisa, puffing a bit from all the exercise. "If this is your first time doing it, don't worry. You'll soon pick it up. It's very easy. Here we go! And one, two, three, four!"

Claire concentrated hard and thought she was doing quite well until from behind her she heard Amelia say, "Doesn't she look funny!" Then Steph giggled.

Claire felt her face getting hot. She didn't know whether Amelia and Steph were talking about her, but it put her off. So when everyone else started galloping to the left, Claire went to the right by mistake. Chris came and stood beside her to help her. Claire knew he was only being kind, but she felt really

stupid, especially when she heard more giggles coming from behind.

It was a big relief when the aerobics class was over.

"Drink and snack time," said another helper called Donna. "Follow me, kids!"

Amelia and Steph ignored her. They were still trying out bits of the routine. Claire went and stood in the queue for drinks. She felt quite lonely just then because everyone else was talking to someone. She was the only one just standing there.

But a moment later she got a shock because Steph and Amelia had crept up right behind her. They both burst out laughing when they saw the surprise on Claire's face.

As Claire turned back round again she caught sight of Nick talking to a really

pretty girl at the door. She had loads of sparkling clips in her hair, and she was wearing a glittery, silver belt. Nick was pointing in Claire's direction.

Amelia and Steph must have noticed her too. "She's pretty," said Amelia.

"Yeah, and cool," said Steph. "I hope she stays, then we can make friends with her."

"Did you see that?" said Amelia. "She smiled at us."

"Yeah, that's because she can tell *we're* cool… Not like you-know-who."

Claire felt her cheeks burning. She'd been sure the girl had smiled at *her*.

"What do you want to drink, Claire? asked Donna.

"Orange squash please," Claire said quietly. Then she looked back at the door. The girl had gone.

"Enjoying yourself?" asked Donna brightly as she poured out the orange squash.

Claire nodded, wondering if it counted as less of a lie because she hadn't actually spoken.

Chapter Six

The water in the swimming pool was lovely and warm. Claire was lying on three floats, staring at the swirly pattern on the ceiling, and listening to her mum laughing as she tried to get away from her dad, who was pretending to be a shark. Through the glass partition Claire could see Lisa putting equipment away.

Lisa happened to glance over and gave Claire a wave. Then a moment later she was on the poolside.

 35

"Are you coming tomorrow, Claire?" she asked with a big smile.

"Er...I'm not sure yet..." said Claire. "I might go out with Mum and Dad."

Her mum and dad had stopped fooling around and were looking quite surprised that Claire didn't seem all that keen on going back the next day. Claire hadn't told them what a horrible time she'd had. She didn't want to talk about it. It just made her feel upset.

"Oh, that's a shame, because someone was asking if you were going to be there."

Huh! I bet that was Amelia or Steph, thought Claire. They probably want another chance to be horrible to me.

"Was it Amelia?" asked Claire, trying to make her voice sound as normal as possible.

"No, it was a girl called Lauren. She

popped in earlier on but she was too late
for this afternoon's session so she's
coming back tomorrow."

Claire remembered the pretty girl at
the door talking to Nick. "Are...are you
sure she meant me?"

"That's what Nick said."

Lisa beamed and Claire felt happier
than she'd felt all day. She didn't want
to get too excited though because Nick
could have got it wrong, and Lauren
might have been smiling at Amelia and
Steph really. But it would be so great to
be friends with Lauren.

"OK, I'll come," said Claire.

"Brilliant!" said Lisa. "See you
tomorrow then!"

The next day at two o'clock Claire
waved goodbye through the window to

her parents, who were off on a hike. They had their rucksacks on their backs and were coming back to collect Claire at teatime.

The moment they were out of sight Claire started to feel worried. What if Lauren decided not to come after all? What if Amelia and Steph were nasty again?

Claire was waiting for a turn on the trampoline. She wished the girl who was having her turn would hurry up and finish, because she didn't want Amelia and Steph to suddenly appear. They'd only put her off and make her do something stupid or clumsy.

Great. The girl was getting off.

"Come on, Claire," said Nick, who was on trampoline duty at that moment. "Up you get. Looks like you might get a

long turn. There's no one waiting."

Claire felt completely different from how she'd felt the day before. She even thought she might try a somersault. She jumped higher and higher and did a few tucks. Then she did alternate sitting and standing bounces.

"You're pretty good at this, aren't you?" said Nick, grinning.

And that made Claire feel even better. Suddenly she decided to be really brave. She did the biggest bounce ever and flung her legs up in the air.

"Look who it is!" said a familiar voice behind her. "Clumsy Claire!"

And Claire froze right in the middle of her great somersault. Then she really did feel clumsy because she landed awkwardly on her side and had to roll over and get up again.

Nick was standing at the other side of the trampoline from Amelia and Steph. He hadn't heard what they'd said because he was right next to one of the speakers and the music was playing quite loudly.

"Are you all right?" he asked Claire. "That was a bit of a funny one, wasn't it!"

Claire went bright red. The only reason she didn't get off was because she wanted to wait till her face had gone back to its usual colour first.

"Hi Lauren," called Nick.

Oh no! thought Claire. Lauren's here. She probably saw me make a mess of that. And now she's going to see my red face too. She'll never want to make friends with me.

"There's that cool girl," said Amelia.

"Let's go and make friends with her. She's looking at us again."

Claire didn't dare turn round. Being careful not to look in Lauren's direction, she climbed down from the trampoline and put on her trainers. This was going to be another horrible afternoon after all. She should never have come to the Kids' Centre.

Chapter Seven

As Claire straightened up, someone spoke.

"Hi, my name's Lauren. Um...are you Claire?"

Claire turned round. Lauren was even prettier close up. She'd spoken in a really gentle voice. Claire wondered if this was what Cinderella felt like when her Fairy Godmother suddenly appeared.

She was suddenly a bit tongue-tied. "Y...yes. Are you...are you...on your own too?"

Lauren nodded. "I saw you in the café yesterday," she said, "and I asked Nick what you were called. I was a bit nervous because I didn't have anyone to come with, and Nick said you were on your own too. I thought you looked really nice and friendly."

Claire felt so happy. She was sure now that she really *was* the one Lauren wanted to be friends with. "What shall we do?" she asked.

"Table tennis?" suggested Lauren.

"I'm not very good at it," said Claire. She was worried about doing anything that might stop Lauren being friends with her.

"Neither am I," said Lauren. "It doesn't matter."

From over in the café, Chris's raised voice made Lauren and Claire look to

see what was happening.

"Right, that's enough, you two! Go and join in with one of the activities."

Amelia and Steph were wrestling with Chris and he was trying to shake them off. They carried on for another few seconds until he sounded really cross. "I mean it! Off! Now!"

That made them stop. Amelia noticed Claire watching her, and stuck out her tongue.

"Just ignore them," said Lauren, walking over to the table-tennis table.

Claire followed her.

"You go first," said Lauren. "You're sure to be better than me!"

Claire and Lauren played table tennis for ages. The ball missed the table more often than not, but it was still brilliant fun. The aerobics class was good fun too,

because there was a new bit when you had to work out a clapping pattern with a partner. Lisa thought Lauren and Claire's was so good that they had to show everyone.

At the end Amelia and Steph came up to Lauren.

"You did the routine really well," said Amelia, smiling.

"Thanks," said Lauren, looking surprised.

Claire couldn't help feeling a little stab of worry. Amelia and Steph were trying to get Lauren to be friends with them instead of her. *What if they succeeded?*

"Are you coming tomorrow?" she asked Lauren, when the two of them were having their snack a few minutes later.

"I can't. We're going to see a show." Lauren wrinkled up her nose. "I wish

you could come too." Then her eyes widened and she spoke in an excited gabble. "I'll ask Mum if you *can*, shall I?"

Claire grinned and nodded hard.

"How shall we get in touch with each other?" asked Lauren.

"Do you know your mum's mobile number?"

"Yes, that's a good idea. I'll write it down."

Then Claire frowned as a horrible thought came into her head. "But what if your mum says I'm not allowed to come?"

"Well you could ask your mum and dad to take you to the show, then we'll see each other anyway!"

"Wicked!" said Claire.

Lauren borrowed a pen and a piece of bright pink paper from Lisa and wrote down the phone number. Claire tucked it

46

in her trousers' pocket, and the two of them went off to join in a game that Donna was organising.

At five o'clock Lauren had to go.

Claire's mum and dad came to collect her at five thirty.

"Guess what?" said Claire, rushing up to her parents the moment they appeared. "I met this girl called Lauren – the one Lisa was talking about. She's my friend now. I've got her mum's mobile number. She's going to ask if I can go to a show with them tomorrow..."

"Whoa! Not so fast!" laughed Claire's dad.

"I said you'd make a new friend, didn't I?" said Claire's mum.

"Yes, but can I go to the show with her?"

"Well we'll need to speak to Lauren's

parents first," said Claire's dad. "Let's talk about it in the morning, shall we?"

"Did you have a good time?" Lisa asked Claire again, as they left the Centre.

"Brilliant!" said Claire.

And this time it wasn't a lie.

Chapter Eight

From the moment she'd woken up, Claire had been pestering her parents to let her phone Lauren.

It wasn't until after breakfast that they agreed.

"I think Mum or I need to have a word with Lauren's mum," said Claire's dad. "What's the number?"

Claire was wearing the same trousers that she'd been wearing the day before. She felt in both pockets but there were no pieces of paper there. Her heart started banging and a little shiver of alarm grazed her body.

"I've lost the bit of paper!" she said in a small voice. "What am I going to do?"

"Let's just check it's not lying around somewhere here."

So the three of them looked in every room in the lodge, but there was no sign of it.

"It's only one day that she can't come to the Centre," said her mum. "It's not the end of the world. You'll see her tomorrow."

"Tomorrow!" said Claire. "But that's ages away." Then Claire had an idea. "*I* know! We could go and see the show that Lauren's going to see with her family. Please say yes!"

Claire's mum and dad looked at each

other. "I'd quite like to see a show," said her mum.

"Yes, why not?" said her dad.

"Brilliant!" said Claire, giving them both a quick hug.

"So what's the name of the show?" asked Claire's mum.

Claire's face fell. "Oh no! Lauren never said."

"Let's go over to reception and have a look at all those leaflets there. If there's a show on in town, it's sure to be advertised somewhere."

A few minutes later Claire and her parents were looking through all the leaflets and flyers on the desk in reception.

"This must be it!" said Claire's mum. "*The Tinderbox*. It's on at the Carlton Theatre."

"What time does it start?" asked Claire, wishing it would say ten o'clock in the morning.

"Two o'clock," said her mum.

Then Claire thought of something else. "Can we stay in the holiday village this morning? We might see Lauren."

"No, definitely not," said her mum. "We're not hanging about when we could be out enjoying ourselves. You'll see her this afternoon."

When quarter to two finally arrived, Claire and her parents were in the foyer of the theatre. They'd bought their tickets and a programme and were watching out for any sign of Lauren. Claire's eyes were darting everywhere. She was desperate for Lauren to appear.

"Maybe they're already sitting in the

auditorium," said Claire's dad. But there was no sign of Lauren anywhere, and by the time the lights went down Claire felt like crying.

The show was really good but Claire couldn't enjoy it. She was worrying that Lauren might think she hadn't phoned because she didn't want to be friends any more. What if Lauren never went to the Centre again? That would be so awful.

"Why don't we go back to the holiday village for a swim," said her dad.

Claire was desperate to get back, but not to go swimming.

"Can I have a look round for Lauren first?"

"I think we'd be wasting our time, love," said her mum. "She could be anywhere. "Why don't we go and have

a nice swim, then it'll be evening time. Tomorrow will be here before you know it!"

Chapter Nine

As Claire got into the swimming pool she could hear the noise from the Kids' Centre on the other side of the partition. It would be nearly going home time. She wondered if Amelia and Steph were there. Then she heard Steph's loud giggle. What a relief it was to be safely in the swimming pool with her mum and dad.

As Claire came up from a handstand and blinked the water from her eyes, she suddenly caught sight of what was going on in the Kids' Centre. Everyone was clustered round the table with the jar of sweets on it. Oh yes, Lisa had said something about announcing the winner at the end of today's session. They all had their backs to the swimming pool but Claire could see Amelia and Steph in the group.

Then she got a shock. Standing right next to Amelia was a girl with lovely long blonde hair. Claire couldn't believe her eyes. It was Lauren.

It can't be! thought Claire. She said she couldn't come... But she wasn't at the show either... I don't understand what's going on...

Then something even more shocking happened. Amelia's arm went round Lauren's shoulder. Claire thought she'd

never felt so sad in all her life. Lauren was *her* friend. What was she doing with those two?

At that moment Lauren shook Amelia's arm off and started looking round. Her eyes met Claire's and she broke into a huge beam as she rushed towards the door that came through to the swimming pool, at the end of the partition. A moment later she was standing on the poolside.

"You're not allowed in here with shoes on!" called Donna, who was on pool duty.

"Sorry!" said Lauren. And with that she took off her trainers and threw them behind her without looking to see where they were going to land. "I thought you were going to phone me!" she said in a hurt voice to Claire.

Claire pulled herself up and out of the pool and started gabbling. "I lost your number and I didn't know what to do, so we went to see *The Tinderbox*, but you weren't there."

"Oh no!" said Lauren. "When you didn't phone I told Mum that I didn't want to go to the show any more and then I really begged her to let me come to the Centre. And I've just been waiting and waiting for you to come. And those two horrible girls have been trying to make friends with me all afternoon and I kept telling them to leave me alone…"

Lauren looked so upset that Claire gave her a big hug.

"Watch out!" called her mum. "You're soaking the poor girl."

Lauren giggled. So did Claire.

"Lisa's just about to announce who won the sweet counting competition," said Lauren. "Let's go and see, quick!"

So Claire dripped her way through to the Kids' Centre, just as two people called out her name.

"Claire! Where are you going?" called Donna after her.

"Claire!" said Lisa. "You've won the prize for guessing the number of sweeties in the jar. Come and collect it before you freeze!"

And as Claire went up for her prize, Amelia and Steph were the only two who didn't clap. Amelia even pulled a horrible face at Claire. But this time Lisa saw.

"I've had enough of you two," she snapped. "It's very bad sportsmanship not to clap the person who's won."

Amelia and Steph both scowled and started clapping very slowly.

When Claire had got her prize she heard Steph say, "Lauren, come and stand with us!"

"No, I'm staying with Claire," replied Lauren.

And Claire felt so happy as she walked back to her new friend, clutching the jar of sweets.

"Oh there's my mum, come to meet me," said Lauren, "Look, she's gone to see if I'm in the swimming pool."

The two girls watched through the glass as Lauren's mum looked quickly over the nearly empty pool. Then she smiled and said something to Claire's mum, who was swimming at that end.

"I bet she's telling her she's looking for me," grinned Lauren. "They might make

friends," she added. Then she knitted her eyebrows as she looked down. "Hey, what's that?"

There was a bit of pink paper on the floor next to the partition. Lauren bent down and picked it up, and when she saw what it was, Claire gasped.

"So *that's* where it went!" she said. "I'm not going to lose it again." She felt for her trousers' pocket, but there was nothing there but wet swimsuit. She looked at Lauren and they both burst out laughing.

"Don't worry," said Lauren. "There'll be loads more chances this week for me to give you the phone number. Look! Mum's got her swimming things. That means we can stay together longer."

"D'you think we'll stay friends when our holiday's over?" asked Claire.

"Course we will!" said Lauren, looking a bit hurt that Claire had thought they might not. "We'll be friends for ever!"

Coming up next in...

Make Friends With
Lauren

She's dreamed of being a film star –
and now **Lauren's** got the look!

Flip me over!

Who will YOU meet next?

Make Friends With books are available from all good bookshops,
or can be ordered direct from the publisher:
Orchard Books, PO BOX 29, Douglas IM99 1BQ
Credit card orders please telephone 01624 836000
or fax 01624 837033
or e-mail: bookshop@enterprise.net for details.

To order please quote title, author and ISBN
and your full name and address.
Cheques and postal orders should be made payable to
'Bookpost plc.'
Postage and packing is FREE within the UK
(overseas customers should add £1.00 per book).

Prices and availability are subject to change.

Make Friends With

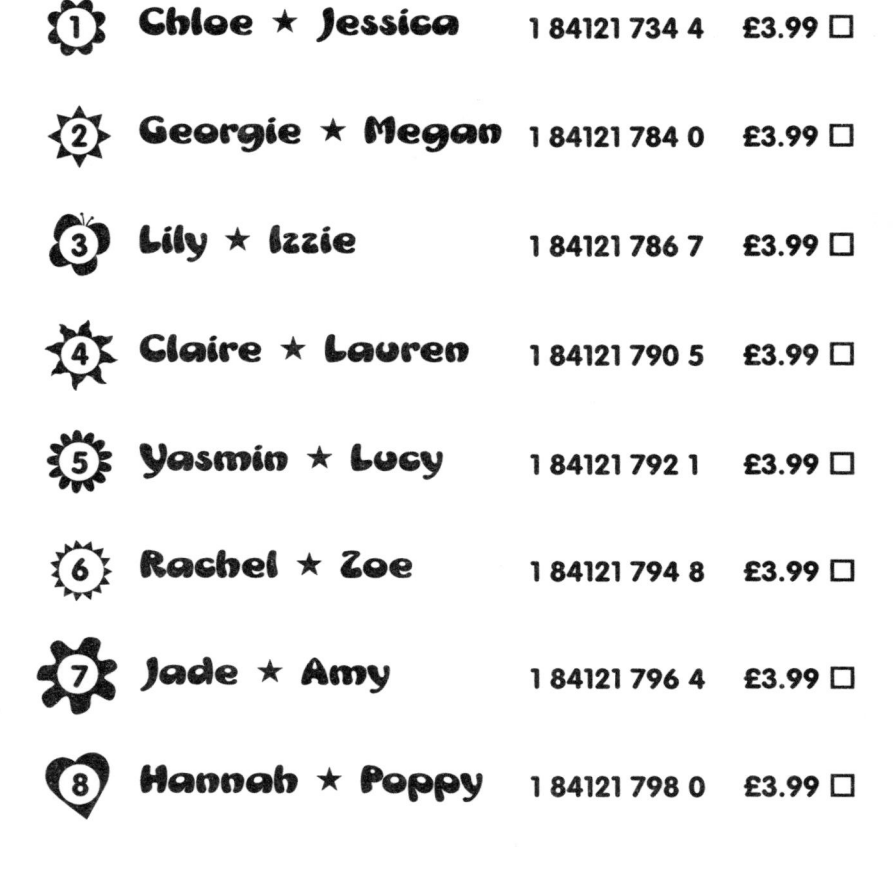

1. **Chloe ★ Jessica**   1 84121 734 4   £3.99 ☐

2. **Georgie ★ Megan**   1 84121 784 0   £3.99 ☐

3. **Lily ★ Izzie**   1 84121 786 7   £3.99 ☐

4. **Claire ★ Lauren**   1 84121 790 5   £3.99 ☐

5. **Yasmin ★ Lucy**   1 84121 792 1   £3.99 ☐

6. **Rachel ★ Zoe**   1 84121 794 8   £3.99 ☐

7. **Jade ★ Amy**   1 84121 796 4   £3.99 ☐

8. **Hannah ★ Poppy**   1 84121 798 0   £3.99 ☐

Look out for...

Make Friends With

Yasmin

**She just wants to have fun – so why is
Yasmin's big brother being so serious?**

Lauren

"Why aren't you being friends?"
asked Lauren.

"I am friends really," Yasmin said.
"Only I've got to pretend that I'm not.
It's all part of my plan, you see."

Lauren was puzzled. "What do
you mean?"

For Rachel Smith, my faithful reader.
Enjoy your favourite book in the series!

Make Friends with

Lauren

Ann Bryant

ORCHARD BOOKS

Chapter One

It was very late on Saturday night.
Lauren was lying in bed listening to
every little sound. The babysitter had
gone downstairs ages ago but Lauren
didn't feel at all tired. It was her mum
and step-dad's wedding anniversary and
they'd gone out for a candlelit dinner.
Lauren thought it was very romantic.
Before they'd set off, her step-dad,
Trevor, had let Lauren into a secret.

"I've got a special present for your

mum," he'd whispered to Lauren. "I'm going to give it to her in the restaurant."

Lauren couldn't wait to see what the present was. Her mum was lucky. She'd have that same lovely feeling that Lauren had got when her friend Claire gave her a present at the end of their holiday. Lauren and Claire had become great friends during the holiday. And the bracelet of five glittery strands that Claire had given her had been such a brilliant surprise.

A car drew up outside. Lauren listened hard. A door banged. Then another. Yes!

The next thing Lauren heard was the front door opening and voices downstairs. Then a minute later the front door shut and the car engine started up. That would be Trevor taking the babysitter home. As the car pulled away,

Lauren's mum's footsteps sounded on the stairs.

"What was Trevor's present?" asked Lauren, sitting bolt upright the very second the bedroom door opened.

Her mum got a shock. "Oh! You're awake! It's very late, young lady!"

Lauren gasped. Round her mum's neck, sparkling and glittering in the shadowy light, was the most beautiful necklace. It looked as though it should belong to a film star.

"Wow!" breathed Lauren, getting out of bed to have a proper look.

Her mum smiled as she fingered the necklace. "I know!" she said. "I couldn't believe it when I opened the case."

"It must have cost a lot of money!" said Lauren. "Can I try it on?"

"You can in the morning," said her

7

mum. "As long as you go to sleep now."

When she'd gone out Lauren closed her eyes and pictured the necklace. Then she started imagining herself wearing it, and everyone looking at her, thinking *she* was a film star. And after a bit the daydreams turned into real dreams.

The first thing Lauren thought about when she woke up was the necklace. Her mum and Trevor were downstairs. She could hear their voices. So she rushed into their bedroom and opened the top drawer of the dressing-table. A long slim case lay on top of her mum's big jewellery box. Lauren guessed this would be it. She opened the case and touched the silver chain. It felt cold and precious. She lifted one end of it and watched the bright stones twist and glint. And that was when

she noticed a little heart on the back of the chain with the letters A M on it.

"Lauren! What are you doing?"

"I was only looking," said Lauren, going red at the sound of her mum's voice behind her, because she knew she shouldn't really be going through her mum's things.

"Well, you ought to have asked first."

"Sorry... What are these letters here?"

Lauren's mum's face broke into a smile. "My initials – A M – for Anne McCrae. Trevor asked the jeweller to inscribe them in this little heart to make the necklace even more special. Wasn't that sweet of him?"

Lauren thought it was very romantic. "Can I try it on?"

Her mum helped her with the clasp at the back, then Lauren stared at herself in

the mirror for ages. The necklace looked amazing! If only her friends could see her wearing it. They'd be so impressed.

"Will you take it to work to show everyone, Mum?"

Her mum laughed. "I don't know about that. But I'm certainly going to wear it next Saturday night at the Johnsons' party."

"You'll be the most beautiful lady there," said Lauren, giving her mum a hug.

"The trouble is, the necklace is too good for any clothes I've got, so I'm going to have to buy a new dress to go with it!"

"Buy a blue one. That'd look brilliant!" said Lauren.

For the rest of the day, Lauren couldn't

stop thinking about the necklace. Three times she asked her mum if she could go and have a look at it. The third time her mum sighed and looked a bit fed up. So the fourth time she decided it might be better not to ask again, in case she said no.

Her mum and Trevor were watching something on television. Lauren slipped out of the room and tiptoed upstairs and into her mum's room. This time she didn't take the necklace out of its case. She just looked at it thoughtfully, then closed the case again. An idea had come into Lauren's head. She carefully moved the case until the side of it was exactly lined up with the side of the jewellery box. Then she stared at the case and the box as she thought about her idea.

It was a brilliant idea, but Lauren knew she shouldn't do it.

Chapter Two

The moment Lauren went into the classroom on Monday morning she started to tell her friends about her mum's necklace.

"You should see it!" she said to Alice. "It glitters and sparkles like anything!"

Alice's eyes were sparkling at the thought of it. "She's lucky, your mum."

"Why is she lucky?" said Tilly, who was going past at that moment.

"Because Lauren's step-dad's given her

a beautiful necklace for their wedding anniversary," Alice explained.

Francesca had just arrived. "What are you talking about?" she asked.

So Alice explained again and in the end Lauren was the centre of attention, with everyone talking about her mum's necklace.

"I don't know why you're going on about it so much," said Tilly, looking grumpy. "My mum's got loads of precious jewels and I don't boast about them."

"She wasn't boasting," said Alice, sticking up for Lauren.

Lauren didn't say anything but she wished like mad that she could actually show Tilly Garlick her mum's necklace. Then Tilly would see what she was talking about.

All day long Lauren had to put up with Tilly's comments.

"My mum's got earrings that dangle and sparkle right down to her shoulders... My mum's engagement ring's got five real diamonds *and* a real sapphire in it... My mum's got six precious necklaces and fifteen other ones – and they all glitter – even in the dark!"

By the time Lauren got home, her mind was made up. She was definitely going to carry out her brilliant plan now. First she had to check something, though. She waited till her mum was ironing, then she nipped upstairs.

In the top dressing-table drawer, the side of the slim case was still exactly level with the side of the jewellery box. That showed that her mum hadn't taken her

necklace out of its case. Lauren hugged herself with excitement. She knew now that her plan would work because her mum would never notice that the necklace was missing, if Lauren left its case in the drawer. Not just for one little day…

After breakfast, the next morning Lauren sneaked into her mum and Trevor's room and took the necklace out of its case. Her heart was beating like mad when she put it on. She shivered as the cold chain rested against her skin under her school shirt and sweatshirt.

When she got into the classroom, Lauren went straight to Alice. "Look!" she whispered, her eyes shining, as she undid the top shirt button and pulled down the neck of her sweatshirt.

Alice gasped. "It's so cool!" she breathed. "Show Tilly!" Alice grinned at Lauren. "I can't wait to see the look on her face!"

Tilly was in the middle of a group of friends in the library corner.

"Lauren's got something to show you!" said Alice excitedly.

"What?" asked Tilly.

Lauren didn't reply. She just pulled the top of the sweatshirt down again.

"Oh wow!" said two or three girls. "It's beautiful."

"Yeah, it's wicked!" said a girl called Anna.

"It's amazing that your mum let you bring it to school!" said Yasmin.

Lauren didn't say anything.

Tilly had picked up a book. She started turning the pages slowly. "I don't

think it's anything special," she said in a bored-sounding voice. "In fact my mum's got one just like it."

"I bet she hasn't!" said Alice, her eyes flashing.

"Well, you bet wrong," said Tilly.

"You're making it up because you're jealous of Lauren," said Alice.

And one or two girls mumbled, "Yes, she's just jealous."

"They're really common, actually," Tilly went on, in her bored voice. "My mum doesn't bother to wear hers any more because it's so old-fashioned. In fact, she lets me borrow it for dressing-up whenever I want."

There was a short silence. Quite a few of the girls were looking impressed.

"Hey, lucky thing!" said Anna. "I wish I could borrow *my* mum's jewellery."

Tilly smiled at Anna, then rolled her eyes like a grown-up. "It's no big deal!" she said.

"If she lets you borrow it whenever you want, why don't you bring it to school?" asked Francesca, looking excited.

Tilly kept turning the pages of her book, with a bored look on her face. Everybody was watching her, wondering what she'd say.

"Yeah, why don't you?" asked Alice.

"Tilly still didn't look up – just drawled, "OK, I'll bring it tomorrow."

Lauren quickly did up her top button. She felt silly now she knew Tilly's mum had got one too. The necklace obviously wasn't anything special after all.

Chapter Three

That afternoon it was Outdoor Games.

"Don't take it off," whispered Alice when they were getting changed. "It might get lost."

But when Lauren had changed into her PE shirt and shorts, the necklace showed. It was hidden, but the top of the shirt looked kind of bumpy.

"What have you got under there, Lauren?" asked Miss Sharman, who always took them for Games.

"Nothing," said Lauren, her heart thumping.

Miss Sharman frowned and was about to peer more closely, when another teacher appeared and started talking to her.

Alice quickly undid the clasp and told Lauren to stuff the necklace into the toe of her sock. "And put your sock into your shoe," she added.

"And your shoe under your sweatshirt," said Yasmin. "Then it'll be safe."

"Now, where was I?" said Miss Sharman when she'd finished talking to the other teacher. "Oh yes..." Her eyes went straight to Lauren's PE shirt. A puzzled look came over her face, then she smiled round at everyone and said, "OK, out you all go. Chop chop!"

Miss Sharman was good at inventing games. Today, she divided the class into

four groups and explained what each group had to do. There were four activities with balls and beanbags, hoops and the netball ring. And you had exactly ten minutes on each before your group moved round to the next one.

"I'm puffed out," said Francesca, who'd gone all red in the face.

Lauren was puffed out too, but she never went red. "That was brilliant!" she said to Alice as they went back to the changing rooms.

They were so busy talking about the Games lesson that neither of them gave the necklace a thought until they'd changed completely back into their school uniforms. Then they both thought about it at the same moment. Lauren turned slowly to Alice, her eyes big and round.

"The necklace!" she said in a shocked

whisper. "It wasn't in my sock!"

"Are you sure you haven't dropped it or something?" asked Alice.

The two of them crouched down and started frantically looking under the benches.

Lauren heaved a big sigh as they slowly straightened up again.

"What's the matter?" asked Yasmin, seeing Lauren's worried face.

"My necklace has gone," said Lauren.

"I'll help you look," said Yasmin.

"Me too," added Francesca.

"Hurry up, you last few girls," said Miss Sharman, walking over from the other side of the changing room. "Stop chatting and go back to your classroom."

"Lauren's lost…" began Francesca.

"…her scrunchie," finished Yasmin.

Lauren's heart was banging against

her ribs. Thank goodness Yasmin had managed to stop Francesca from saying the word "necklace". Lauren knew she'd be in big trouble if any of the teachers found out that she'd brought the necklace to school. You weren't allowed any valuable things in school.

"It's in your hair, you silly thing!" said Miss Sharman, grinning at Lauren. "Go on. Off you all go!"

Francesa went red. "Sorry," she said, as the four girls walked back to the classroom. "I wasn't thinking."

"It's OK," said Lauren.

Alice stopped suddenly and grabbed Lauren's arm. "I bet Tilly's taken it!" she said.

Lauren and Francesca gasped. "*Taken* it!"

"But why?" asked Yasmin.

24

"So she can bring it into school tomorrow and pretend it's her mum's!"

"But when could she have taken it?" Lauren asked.

"During Games!" said Francesca, eyes wide. "I was in the same group as Tilly, and she asked Miss Sharman if she could go to the loo."

"That proves it!" said Alice.

"Let's ask her," said Francesca fiercely.

Yasmin frowned. Lauren bit her lip.

Francesca screwed up her face crossly. "Tell her your mum'll be furious with you," she added.

Lauren felt close to tears. She was dreading talking to Tilly, but she knew she had to do it, because Francesca was right — her mum *would* be furious.

Chapter Four

The classroom was busy and noisy. Everyone was tidying up and getting ready for home time. Mrs Traill, the teacher, was putting some work in the big cupboard. Two of the boys were helping her. Tilly was in her place. Lauren decided to go straight over to her while no one was paying attention. Yasmin, Alice and Francesca followed behind.

"I was wondering if you'd borrowed my mum's necklace?" asked Lauren in

a shaky voice. She specially said "borrowed" because it sounded nicer than "taken".

Tilly looked at her as though she was mad. "What?"

Lauren said it again, in an even shakier voice.

Then Francesca jumped in impatiently, "We know you've got it, Tilly Garlick. So just give it back or we're telling."

"I don't know what you're on about!" said Tilly, giving Francesca a horrible look.

"You went to the loo in Games and that's when you took it," said Alice, sounding much calmer than Francesca.

"How *can* I have taken it when I didn't even know where it was?" asked Tilly, sneering at Alice.

Lauren gulped. Maybe it wasn't Tilly

after all. She hadn't noticed if anyone had been watching when she'd hidden the necklace in her sock, she'd been in such a rush.

"We know you're fibbing," said Francesca. "And Lauren's telling of you. Aren't you, Lauren?"

Lauren nodded glumly.

Tilly smiled a nasty smile. "Tell, then!" she said. "I don't care. The teacher'll only tell *you* off for bringing the necklace to school in the first place, Lauren. And then she'll tell you off even more for accusing people when you can't prove anything, so there!"

Lauren felt as though someone had stamped on her toe really hard. What a terrible mess she was in. Everything had gone wrong. She should never have taken her mum's precious necklace.

Chapter Five

When Lauren and Alice went out at
morning break the next day, the first
thing they noticed was a little crowd
round Tilly Garlick. Francesca, who
was on the outside of the crowd, came
running over.

"Tilly's brought a necklace into
school!" she said, her eyes big and
round with the important news. "I
think it's the same as your mum's!"

"Let's go and look," said Alice,

grabbing Lauren's hand. "I bet it *is* the same. And that will prove she stole yours yesterday!"

Lauren felt sick. Even if Alice was right, there was nothing she could do about it. She wished she could just press a big button that said *REWIND* and find that it had gone back to Monday and she'd never brought the necklace to school at all.

"Look!" hissed Alice in Lauren's ear. "It *is* your mum's. It's exactly the same!"

They were standing on tiptoe at the back of the group. It was true that an identical necklace to Lauren's mum's was dangling from Tilly's hand. It glinted in the sun.

"Didn't your mum mind you bringing it to school?" asked Alice, wide-eyed.

"No," said Tilly. "She's got loads like

this. I told you, I can borrow it whenever I want." At that moment Tilly saw Lauren at the back of the group. "See," she gloated, "I said my mum had got one just the same, didn't I?"

Lauren looked down. She didn't know what to say.

Francesca suddenly blurted out, "Tilly's lying, because Lauren left her necklace in the changing room yesterday. And when she got back from Games, it had disappeared." Francesca's voice rose. "And it must have been Tilly because she was the only person who went to the loo in Games. So there!"

Lauren looked up. She felt a tiny ray of hope because everyone was staring at Tilly. Surely she'd tell the truth now. Lauren thought that at any moment the necklace might be flung down to the

ground, and Tilly might shout out, "OK, have it back!"

But no such thing happened. Tilly didn't look at all angry. In fact her face crumpled like people's faces do when they're just about to burst into tears.

"It's not fair," she said in a whiny voice. "Just because my mum's got one the same, everyone thinks I took Lauren's, and I didn't."

There was a short silence, and a few girls who'd had cross faces, looked suddenly sorry for Tilly. A girl called Nicole put her arm round her. "Leave Tilly alone."

Anna scowled at Lauren. "Yeah, stop being so horrible." Then she led Tilly away.

"Come on, Lauren," said Alice. "Let's go and play over here."

She went marching off in the other direction, Francesca following her. But Lauren felt as though she was rooted to the spot. Yasmin was still standing next to her.

"Do *you* think I'm being horrible to Tilly?" Lauren asked her, in a small voice.

Yasmin shook her head. "I'm sure Tilly's making it up that it's her mum's. But I don't know how we can prove it," she said, looking sorry for Lauren.

Lauren gave Yasmin a sad sort of smile. It was nice of her to be so kind when she wasn't even one of Lauren's best friends.

"Big day tomorrow!" said Lauren's mum at teatime. "I'm going to buy my new dress! Blue! Just like you suggested."

Lauren gulped. She knew her mum would want to try the necklace on with the dress when she got home.

"You don't seem to be yourself, love. Are you feeling all right?"

It was the perfect chance to tell her mum the whole story, but Lauren simply didn't dare. Her mum would be so cross and upset.

"I'm OK."

Lauren went up to her room and began to change out of her school uniform. She was thinking about Tilly showing off with the necklace, and then Yasmin saying how she was sure it couldn't be Tilly's mum's but she didn't know how to prove it.

She chucked her sweatshirt on the bed and caught sight of the name tape. And suddenly something really important hit

her. Of course! Her mum's initials on the little heart! That would prove it! Why ever hadn't she thought of that before?

A few minutes later she was on the phone to Yasmin. Her mum had looked up Yasmin's phone number and said she didn't mind Lauren phoning her as long as she was quick.

Lauren took care to speak really quietly to be quite sure her mum didn't hear. "Hi Yasmin. It's Lauren."

Yasmin sounded really pleased to hear from her. "Oh hi!"

"You know what you said about having to prove it was really my mum's necklace?"

"Yes, I've been thinking about that."

Lauren felt happy that Yasmin was still thinking about it. "Well, I've just remembered something. My mum's

initials – A M – are on the necklace, on a little heart!"

"Hey, brilliant!" Then the brightness fell out of Yasmin's voice. "The trouble is, getting Tilly to bring it back to school."

Lauren sighed a big sigh. Yasmin was right. How ever were they going to persuade Tilly to do that?

"Don't worry," said Yasmin. "I'll think of something."

"OK," said Lauren.

But she didn't feel OK at all.

The next morning everyone in Lauren's family overslept. Lauren got dressed in a big hurry and ate her breakfast at top speed.

Then just as they were about to set off for school, her mum remembered the washing needed to be put out.

"Come on, it won't take a second," she said.

But by the time they'd got everything out on the line, it was nearly ten to nine.

The traffic on the way to school was worse than usual because of some new roadworks. So when Lauren went into the classroom, everyone was doing their numeracy.

"Take out your Maths book," said Mrs Traill, in her usual kind voice.

Lauren whispered "Hi" to Yasmin. Yasmin said "Hi" back but she didn't seem to smile. Lauren couldn't understand it. She and Yasmin had been getting on so well yesterday. Yasmin had seemed really friendly.

All through Maths she kept throwing glances at Yasmin, but Yasmin wasn't looking.

By the time the bell went for playtime,
Lauren was desperate to find out if
something was wrong. But there was no
chance because Yasmin shot outside. And
she wasn't on her own. At her side,
grinning and chatting, was Tilly Garlick.

Chapter Six

That playtime was awful. Lauren felt
more lonely and sad than she'd ever felt
before. She joined in Alice's and
Francesca's game, but she couldn't stop
looking over at Yasmin and Tilly who
were sitting on the climbing frame
talking and laughing together.

"What's up with Yasmin?" asked
Alice, in a soft voice.

Lauren shrugged. "Dunno."

She had to pretend she wasn't bothered

because she didn't want people to stare at her or feel sorry for her. But inside she was really hurting. It had been bad enough when she'd only got the problem of the missing necklace, but now that she'd lost the one friend who was going to try and help her solve the problem, everything was twice as bad.

In the afternoon it was Art in the new Art and Craft room. When everyone had started work, Mrs Traill realised she'd left the glue in the classroom. She asked Lauren to go back for it.

It felt strange walking along the corridor during lesson time when the school was so quiet. Lauren found the glue and was about to make her way back to the Art and Craft room, when who should come into the classroom but Yasmin.

"I've got to be quick," said Yasmin. "I wanted to talk to you so I told Mrs Traill I was going to the loo."

"Why aren't you friends?" asked Lauren, feeling relieved that at least Yasmin was talking to her now.

"I *am* friends really. Only I'm pretending to Tilly that I'm not. It's my plan, you see."

Lauren was puzzled. "What do you mean?"

"I've told Tilly I believe her about the necklace." Yasmin gabbled excitedly. "I said I really really loved it, and that she was so lucky. Then I asked if she could bring it in to school again so I could try it on. She said I couldn't try it on, because her mum only let *her* borrow it, but I could look at it."

Lauren gasped. "So is she going to

bring it into school tomorrow?"

"Yes, and if I see your mum's initials on the little heart I'll show her it and tell her that proves it's yours really. I'll tell her it's bad to lie like that, and then she'll have to admit she was wrong and give it you back."

Lauren couldn't believe her ears. A smile began to spread over her face. "I thought you didn't like me any more," she said quietly.

"I know. I've been trying to find a time to talk to you all day, but Tilly was always looking. That's why I came to find you now. You see, when lessons started and you still weren't at school, I thought you weren't coming. Then Tilly needed a rubber, and the whole plan just popped into my head. I let her borrow mine and started being really nice to her."

Yasmin had been talking so much that neither of the girls had noticed the classroom door opening.

It was Miss Sharman. "What's going on here?" she asked, narrowing her eyes suspiciously.

"We're just getting something for Mrs Traill," Lauren said.

"Hurry up then," said Miss Sharman before she disappeared.

"I'll phone you later," whispered Yasmin.

As Lauren got into her mum's car after school she felt happy because of Yasmin being friends again. But then a moment later she remembered that this was the day her mum was buying the new dress. And instantly the happy feeling disappeared and a worried feeling took its place.

"Did you have a nice day?" asked her mum.

"It was all right," said Lauren softly. "Did you?"

"Not bad," said her mum.

Then Lauren spoke in scarcely more than a whisper. "Did you find a dress?"

"Sort of. You see, I *found* the perfect dress but I didn't buy it because I thought it was a bit expensive. Only now I wish I had bought it! In fact I've decided to go back and get it tomorrow before work."

Lauren's mum smiled through the driving mirror and Lauren smiled back, as she heaved a big silent sigh of relief. She could be happy again now. But only just.

She still needed to get the necklace back.

44

Chapter Seven

There were butterflies in Lauren's stomach on the way to school the next day. And her head was full of "what ifs". The biggest one was, *what if Tilly hasn't brought the necklace?*

On the phone the night before, Yasmin had said it was best if she kept on pretending not to be friends with Lauren. Otherwise Tilly might not show her the necklace. But she said she'd give a special signal to tell Lauren whether or

45

not there was a heart with the initials
A M on it, on Tilly's necklace. If Yasmin
scratched the top of her *right* arm it
meant that she *had* seen them on the
necklace. But if she scratched the top of
her *left* arm it meant they *weren't* on the
necklace.

Lauren's butterflies got worse as she went
into the classroom. She saw Yasmin
straight away. She was in the library
corner talking to Tilly. As Lauren sat in
her place, Francesca came over to talk
to her.

"Will you be on my team in Games?"

Lauren nodded and glanced across to
see if Yasmin was giving her any signals.

"If it's partners will you be mine?"
asked Francesca.

"OK," said Lauren, who wasn't really

paying attention because she was so busy trying to watch Yasmin and Tilly out of the corner of her eye.

A second later she got a shock because Yasmin was scratching her arm. But which arm? Lauren tried to work out which arm it was. She thought it was the right arm, but it had all happened so quickly and it was difficult to work out which arm was which when someone was facing you.

The more Lauren thought about it, the more mixed up she got. In the end she even forgot if it was supposed to be the arm of the hand that was doing the scratching or the arm that was being scratched.

"Line up for assembly now please, everyone," said Mrs Traill.

Tilly went over to her place to get her

hymn book. Lauren was desperate to get near enough to Yasmin to ask her in a whisper whether or not she'd seen the heart and the initials on Tilly's necklace. She got her hymn book and went past Yasmin's desk really slowly. And just then Francesca happened to move so she was standing in exactly the right place to block Lauren from Tilly's view. She had to be quick.

"Did you see it?" she hissed at Yasmin.

Yasmin checked Tilly wasn't watching then nodded, looking excited.

But then Francesca spoke in her usual loud voice. "Did you see *what*?"

Tilly immediately looked over.

"Nothing," said Lauren, feeling her face going pink.

"Oh come on," said Francesca. "Tell me what you and Yasmin were just

whispering about."

Lauren wished that the roof would float off and a magic carpet would lower itself into the classroom. Then she could climb on to the carpet and fly away to the other side of the world.

But the roof stayed firmly in place and Lauren's pink face turned pale, as Tilly narrowed her eyes suspiciously and mouthed "I hate you" at Yasmin.

Chapter Eight

It was morning break. In the playground Tilly was playing with Anna and Nicole. As soon as she saw Lauren and Yasmin coming out, she started scowling and whispering.

"She's talking about us," said Lauren.

"I don't care," said Yasmin. "Come on."

She grabbed Lauren's hand and went striding over to Tilly.

"I think you'd better give Lauren her necklace back!" she said in a very

grown-up voice.

Lauren gasped. Alice and Francesca
and a few of the others were coming over
to see what was going on. Lauren felt like
a frozen statue, too scared to speak.

"It's not Lauren's. It's mine!" said Tilly.

"Stop telling lies!" shouted Yasmin.

"I'm not!" Tilly shouted back. "It's
mine!"

"*What's* yours, Tilly?"

Everybody froze. Miss Sharman was
on break duty and she'd come over
without anyone even noticing.

Tilly looked down.

"*What's* yours, Tilly?" repeated Miss
Sharman.

Tilly didn't say anything but her fingers
went up to her neck and she felt for the
necklace through her school sweatshirt.

Miss Sharman's eyes narrowed. "If I'm

not very much mistaken, this is the second time I've seen something bumpy-looking under someone's shirt this week!" Lauren went pale as Miss Sharman's suspicious gaze fell on her. Then the teacher's eyes went back to Tilly. "Let's have a look, Tilly."

Tilly scowled and kept very still.

"Did you hear me, Tilly?"

Very slowly, Tilly reached round the back of her neck and undid the clasp.

"I only brought it to school because everyone wanted me to," she said in a sulky voice, as she plonked the necklace into Miss Sharman's outstretched hand.

"It's not Tilly's. It belongs to Lauren's mum," said Yasmin quietly.

"Lauren's mum!" said Miss Sharman.

"No it doesn't, it's *my* mum's," said Tilly.

"We can prove it," said Yasmin.

Miss Sharman frowned hard at Yasmin. "Go on," she said in a low voice.

"It's got Lauren's mum's initials, A M, in a little heart on it. It was her wedding anniversary present. Lauren brought it to school to show us, and Tilly started boasting that her mum had got one just like it."

Miss Sharman examined the chain. Everyone held their breath. "Yes, the initials A M are engraved here... I can see them in the little heart."

"They're my mum's initials – Anne McCrae," said Lauren quietly.

"So how did the necklace come to be in your hands, Tilly?" asked Miss Sharman.

By this time an even bigger crowd had gathered to see what was going on.

53

"She stole…" began Francesca.

"I'm asking Tilly," interrupted Miss Sharman.

"Dunno," said Tilly.

"That's not good enough, Tilly. You must know."

Tilly began squirming around and her face went very red. "I didn't realise…" she began.

"I want to know how it came to be in your hands, Tilly," said Miss Sharman, in a very stern voice.

Tilly was silent. Everyone was silent. You could have heard an eye blink.

"Well?" said Miss Sharman, tipping her head to one side.

Tilly spoke so quietly, it was almost impossible to hear her. "I took it out of Lauren's sock during Games."

A gasp went round the circle and Miss

Sharman looked up and suddenly realised how many people were standing there listening.

"Off you go! Shoo! Right now!"

And lots of people scuttled away until there was just Lauren, Yasmin, Tilly and Anna standing there with Miss Sharman.

Lauren was full of a lovely feeling of relief that she didn't have to worry about getting the necklace back any more. But the lovely feeling turned into a horrible shock when Miss Sharman suddenly swung round to her, and spoke in an angry voice.

"What a lot of upset, you've caused, Lauren! It was utterly thoughtless of you to bring your mother's precious necklace into school. Did you even ask her permission?"

Lauren shook her head. Tears filled her eyes.

"If you hadn't done such a stupid thing in the first place, then Tilly would never have been tempted to take it."

A sob came into Lauren's throat, and she knew she would have burst into tears if Yasmin hadn't reached out and held her hand just then.

Miss Sharman turned back to Tilly. "But all the same you should *never* steal another person's property, Tilly. And you most certainly shouldn't lie about it."

Lauren and Tilly both looked down.

"I'm going to keep this necklace in a safe place until the end of the day, then you can take it home and give it back to your mother, Lauren." Miss Sharman's eyes went from Lauren to Tilly to Lauren to Tilly. "I hope you've both learnt a lesson from this... Now, Tilly, I want you to say a big sorry to Lauren."

There was another silence.

"I'm waiting, Tilly," said Miss Sharman, in an icy voice.

Tilly spoke in a whisper. "Sorry."

Miss Sharman's words rang in Lauren's ears… *If you hadn't done such a stupid thing in the first place, then Tilly would never have been tempted to take it.*

Lauren saw the tears in Tilly's eyes and managed to give her a very shaky smile. "It's OK," she said.

And then the bell went.

Chapter Nine

It was Saturday night. Lauren and Yasmin were eating pizza as they watched their favourite programme on television.

"What do you think?" said Lauren's mum.

Both girls turned round and gasped.

"Cool!" breathed Yasmin.

Lauren couldn't speak. She'd never seen her mum looking so pretty. Her shoes were bright blue with very high

heels. Her dress was the same colour, soft and shimmery. And the necklace sparkled more brightly than ever before.

"Does she look gorgeous or what?" said Trevor, coming in at that moment.

"Gorgeous," agreed Lauren. "Especially wearing that necklace."

"Don't you go getting ideas, young lady," said Trevor. "It's your mum's necklace you know. You're not to go borrowing it!"

Lauren froze. "I know!" she said, in a high-pitched squeak, her heart beating wildly.

Lauren's mum and Trevor exchanged a puzzled look.

"Why are you looking so worried?" asked Trevor, studying Lauren's face carefully.

"I... I... I...wasn't..."

"Oh yes, you were," said Lauren's mum, narrowing her eyes suspiciously. "You wouldn't ever think of taking something precious like this to show your friends, or anything, would you, love?"

Lauren gulped. She was just wondering what to say when the doorbell rang.

"That'll be the babysitter," said Trevor. "I'll let her in."

"I'd better get my coat and bag," said Lauren's mum. "I didn't realise it was getting so late."

Lauren let out a big sigh of relief the moment her mum and Trevor had gone out of the room. "I nearly got told off all over again," she said to Yasmin.

Yasmin smiled. "You've had enough telling off from Miss Sharman." Lauren gave Yasmin a quick hug for making her feel better.

Then Yasmin's eyes lit up. "That necklace makes your mum looks like a film star, doesn't it?"

"I know!" said Lauren. "That's what made me want to take it into school and show everyone in the first place."

"Oh no!" giggled Yasmin. "You'd better forget I said that then. I don't want you to go and do it again!"

And then the babysitter walked in.

"Hello, you two," she said brightly. "Doesn't your mum look lovely, Lauren? Just like a film star!"

And to the babysitter's surprise, Lauren and Yasmin burst out laughing.